Holly Hustle: Innocence Lost

By

Naughty Tommy

Dedicated to Eduardo

Facebook/NaughtyTommy
Twitter/NaughtyTommy
Tumblr/NaughtyTommy

Disclaimer

All rights reserved.

Table of Contents

Chapter One – Cut!

"C'mon Son…Try it…I know, you love chocolate…So, you'll like it."

"If you ever tell my Mom…I'll kill you…I swear!"

"Ohh, who's the big boy now? That's it…unzip my trousers…Yeah, you've been begging to see what your Step-Daddy is giving your Mamma nightly…You're doing really good job…Just watch the teeth, Son."

Jake's tongue swirled around Floyd's growing black dickhead like a pro; while Floyd gripped the high-top dresser, where a high school football trophy prop was on displayed.

"You see…I told you so…" spoke Floyd.

Squatting in front of this past-his-prime, prima donna, trimmed-short, gray-haired, black muscled Floyd; Jake felt it strange to be licking a cock. Obviously, Jake sucked cock, which normally ended with a cash bill sliding into his front pocket after his customer's satisfaction.

And definitely not in front of four porn production members; especially that overfriendly, gropy Costume Designer/Make-Up Artist, Mario, who sidetracked Jake with his alluring candy and Floyd's pearly-white smile encouragement.

Jake's mouth opened wide as possible, while Floyd's famed python dick started sliding inside. Jake felt Floyd's hands on the back of his head as Floyd's dick descended into Jake's gullet.

"C'mon, Son…Take your Daddy's cock…Make your Daddy proud."

Jake choked on Floyd's cock, but continued with a financial promise.

For a newcomer, and West Hollywood street hustler; Jake finally was getting into it. Taking Floyd's enormous cock would definitely give Jake more prospects…besides more money, once Floyd had fucked his ass.

"Yeah…Make your Daddy's cock harder…That's it! That's my, Son!"

Jake snickered at the clichéd dialogue this old-fart with a black barracuda dick was given. Heck, Floyd was old enough to be Jake's grandpa! Jake was in his prime at twenty-three, while Floyd looked sixtyish?

Floyd looked down furiously.

Who the fuck does He think he is? thought Floyd.

I'll show him to respect his elders.

No street-corner, pretty-boy whore is going to insult the King!

The King, who built this shithouse of a porn studio, which was named in honor of me!

Hell, I wasn't known as MAGNUM for nothing!

Floyd's heavy bull-sized, shaved balls tighten. Floyd knew he was close to cuming, which the production crew anticipated after Floyd had fucked Jake. After plunging Jake's butthole, Floyd unroll the condom, then blast his cumload over Jake's puffy ass lips. Which was known in the porn biz as the creampie shot.

This scene was the money-maker for Sal Falconi's rut of a Studio production, loosely titled "Daddy Knows Best, Part Thirty-One".

Therefore, when Floyd clutched Jake's head harder; maintaining his cock in Jake's mouth; this caused the street-hustler to fret.

Then it happened.

Floyd, the pornstar known as Magnum, unleashed the first wave of cum down Jake's throat without warning and unscripted.

Jake started to panic-gag as his arms waved. Nevertheless, Floyd's firm grasp made Jake swallow it completely. Floyd kept squirting until he had drained his cock inside Jake's pretty-boy mouth. Eventually, Floyd witnessed Jake's distraught tears, running down his cheekbone.

"Damn, Son…You're a good cocksucker…I loved cuming in your warm mouth…And now, for that virgin ass of yours!"

The entire crew heard a popping sounding as Jake's mouth withdrew from Floyd's cock.

"You, son of a bitch! You weren't supposed to unload your cum in my mouth…That wasn't in the contract…God knows if you're safe or not…Hell, I don't even allow my clients, to do that."

"Sorry Jake, but Sweetie…It felt too good to resist…Now get ready for my cock up your hole…"

"Fuck you!"

"Ohh, yeah? You see that Cameraman…He's waiting for my cock to slid inside your pretty little ass…Along with that Photographer…And Our esteemed Director…Now, get on all-fours…Cuz, your ass will get the fill-up of a lifetime!"

"You're an asshole…That's it…I'm out of here…Sal, where's my money?"

This provoked Floyd's notorious temperament.

Floyd shoved Jake against the wall of the studio set, which was a replica of a teenage boy's bedroom. The centerfold model and rock band posters flew off from the force, while the football trophy shattered on the floor. Hell, even parts of the particle board wall had started to fail.

Next, Floyd positioned his bulging-veiny arm against Jake's throat; cutting off Jake's airways as his eyes bulged like a fish out-of-water.

Staring into Jake's panic-stricken eyes, Floyd murmured in a close proximity, "Shut the fuck up…We both know you liked it…Or you would have spat it up by now! Go, strip your clothes off and lick my cock clean."

Terrified and unnerved, Jake's fingers could hardly start undressing his clothes. Ultimately, Floyd ripped off Jake's shirt, then tugged off Jake's snug jeans; leaving Jake wearing a newly purchased jockstrap as Floyd pushed Jack onto the bed.

Meanwhile, the Cameraman and jittery Photographer filmed away.

As their Director stood, concerned about what would happen next; Sal Falconi felt sexually enticed as he stood jerking his raging hardon through his pants. Sal had a fetish for fucking young studs in a jockstrap!

"You see I knew you would like it…Ain't that right, Sal?" spoke Floyd with his last line aimed directly at Sal with a fiendish grin.

As the Owner and Principal Director of Magnum Studio, Sal Falconi knew it was time to cut Floyd from his dwindling talent roster; if you could say having rounded-up Jake on a street corner was an actors list?

This steroid-infused bulging vein muscled; over-aged freak tapped his black dickhead upon this street hustler's cheeky white ass lips as the poor boy started to whimper, waiting to be rescued.

Surprisingly, during their brief script reading, these two "stars" had the perfect chemistry; then Floyd asked their Costume Designer, Mario, to give Jake something to calm his nerves.

Fucking drugs! thought Sal Falconi.

Mr Falconi had lectured Floyd, more times than they had made films together.

Now, it was time to end this train wreck!

With Jake on all-fours, posed on the mattress; Floyd had slithered his dick past Jake's outer ass ring. Floyd's heavily lubed-up cock commenced a bareback thrust session to behold; which went against Magnum Studio's safety policy. Nonetheless, Floyd looked like a bull-rider, gripping Jake's jockstrap waistband as he roared.

"Shit…It hurts! Get him off of me!" howled Jake.

"Just relax, Son…The pain will soon go away."

After a moment, Jake's asshole searing pain had faded, and was replaced with a lustful sensation that caused his buttocks to match each thrust from Floyd's dick.

Meanwhile, Mr Falconi's tenting pants tapping against his still Photographer's shoulder as he approached the set.

Sal wanted the courage to yell, "Cut!"

However, the unthinkable occurred as Jake uttered, "Fuck me."

Floyd slammed his cock deeper as his balls smacked Jake's dimpled ass. Now, Jake's tears of fright were evaporating. Jake now desired Floyd, and all bets were off as Jake continued.

"Ohh…Daddy."

"You like that? Having Daddy's raw cock up your hole…Don't you, Son?"

"God yes…I want you to breed my hole…Give it all to me, Daddy."

Suddenly, Floyd withdrew his dick from Jake's amazingly receptive hole that was stretched-opened, beyond belief.

Again, impromptu; Floyd spoke, "Come here."

That's when, Floyd placed Jake's back against the set wall and lifted Jake up like a rag doll. Jake took the hint from Floyd's bloodshot eyes as he sank his ass on Floyd's immense, cylindrical cock. Jake wrapped his legs around Floyd, while Floyd penetrated Jake's ass triumphantly.

Floyd touted, "Ohh, Son…Your ass feels amazing…See, I told you so!"

Floyd's wrecking-ball onslaught would inevitably cost Sal thousands to keep Jake silent, while tending to his medical bills as Floyd's irrational fuck scene caused the set framing to collapse upon them, hence ending production and nearly closing Magnum Studio for good.

Sure, this horndog of a Director had spewed his junk inside his pants before Floyd's neglectful action caused this disaster. As Sal Falconi left Jake's hospital bedside; it was evident to fire Floyd, once and for all.

Fuck him! pondered Sal.

What has Floyd done for you lately?

But dragged your Studio into his own egotistical fiasco.

It was time to cut Floyd loose.

And change the locks on the doors!

And hire private security, immediately!

Chapter Two – Innocence Discovered

Weeks later, confined in Hawk's Gym mirrored corner, Sal gripped a dumbbell set. The humiliated Owner a West Hollywood foundering gay porn studio, frantically needed a golden ticket like this Kid next to him. Luckily for Sal, his former mega-star had been expelled from this gym.

Sal gazed at this buffed teenage Kid, whose body and looks were flawless.

The Kid even had a dangling sweat droplet on his perky exposed nipple that eventually plummeted to the floor; as if taunting Sal.

Fuck me! What a tease, thought Sal as his dick stirred at the sight.

Hawk's Gym was known as the most affluent and cruisiest West Hollywood gym. Hence the Italian-burly Sal Falconi had to keep-up appearances; for the sake of his doomed MAGNUM Studio. Nonetheless, Sal observed every taut muscle of this tanned eighteen-year-old Kid.

Hell, this Kid was barely old enough to be in here, which got Sal thinking.

Fortunately, the two were weight-lifting in a cramped corner, where the dumbbells sets were racked. Walled by mirrors, Sal had the perfect observation of this Kid's prominent pecs and fuckable bubble butt, to himself. Which made Sal's cock awaken like a beast from slumber.

Fuck! I can't help it, thought Sal as his shaft magnified to nine inches.

Hell, this Kid wore a provocative string tank top, that flaunted his hardened nipples; and that skintight retro 80's gym shorts with the split on the sides, revealing the Kid's peach fuzz covered butt cheeks. Moreover, the Kid's butthole was scantly covered by a pink teasing thong, that displayed itself whenever the Kid bent over.

The Kid, known as Tyler, was the youngest member of Hawk's Gym. Rumored had it; that Tyler developed his incredible muscle definition from years of working as stock boy at the local market, and that one generous member had paid for his yearly membership, in cash.

Talk about having a benefactor? thought Sal, whose brain never stopped thinking about his next fuck nor his business' opportunity.

Whatever the case, Tyler's ample and smooth pecs caused guys to stare as their mouth's salivated, while Tyler's ripe firm ass initiated numerous jack-off daydream sessions in the Sauna and the Showers. Astoundingly, this all happened within Tyler's first week at Hawk's Gym.

Nevertheless, all this admiration was oblivious to Tyler, whose gym routine made him unaware of his surroundings. That was until Tyler's eyes met Mr Falconi's in the mirror reflection, that ignited a spark.

Naturally, they made the usual courteous nods as they exercised in the furthest corner, away from meddling members. Therefore, Sal blatantly gripped his sizeable crotch; while his tongue circled around his sinfully seductive three-day stubble growth, and his juicy lips.

This singular gesture sent a shockwave throughout Tyler's bod, which included his virgin butthole. Tyler's hole clenched at the thought of this manly Daddy cock sliding deep inside his longing asshole; hence, replacing his customary index finger and that secretly hidden bedside dildo.

You bet, Tyler had his share of girls and guys approaching him persistently. However, upon seeing this gentleman's ballooning cock feet away from him; made Tyler excitable, nervous and horny as hell.

The sight of Sal's hard nine inches caused Tyler's own dickhead to intensify on the gym floor for the first-time ever, stretching his pink thong pouch to its limitations as Tyler's breathing amplified.

What the fuck? thought Tyler to himself.

No one can see me like this…

I look like a perv!

With my dick poking my shorts…

Tyler stood, continuing his bicep-curl with the weight rack in front of him as his dick started protruding outwardly with aroused impulses.

"Hey, aren't you new here?" spoke Sal as he approached beside Tyler; practically startling Tyler as Sal dropped-off the dumbbell weights with a thud.

Sal continued speaking with a wink "That's a mighty impressive muscle you got there...And, I'm not talking about your biceps, Kiddo."

Nonetheless, Sal took this opportunity to survey Tyler's beautiful bubble butt with those cute visible ass cheeks, pleading for attention.

"Thank you, Sir...Name's Tyler," said Tyler as his biceps flexed his last set before Tyler re-racked the weights.

Sal spoke, "Sal Falconi, pleasure to meet you, Tyler...But you can call me, Sal...Now, if you don't mind me asking? Are you mature enough to be in here? Because this place was designed with consenting adults in mind. And, you look pretty young."

"Nice to meet you, Sal...I just turned eighteen last week...I work a couple of blocks away at Growers Market...So, I thought why not come in and look around...After my first tour, I was hooked...Especially after hearing that an anonymous donor paid for my first year's membership in full...Isn't that amazing?" said Tyler with his dimple, winning smile.

All the while Sal thought, Yeah, that donor just wants to fuck your ass.

Don't you realize that, Tyler?

"Well, I can see why," spoke Mr Falconi, observing Tyler's hardening dick as Sal stood next to Tyler's shoulder, and continued speaking in a whispering tone, "Don't be shy…It's nothing to be ashamed of…It happens to all of us here…And some more than others…You do like what you see…Don't ya?"

Tyler nodded YES.

With the closeness of Sal's hairy chest emitting heat and his cockhead having ejected from his waistband; Tyler gawked at the spectacle of Mr Falconi's dickhead, trickling pearly jizz. Tyler had never seen another guy's spunk before.

God, I want to taste that, thought Tyler.

Then Tyler's eyes rose upwardly, viewing Mr Falconi's devilish smile.

Sal continued speaking, "May I touch it? There's no need to be shy."

Before Tyler comprehended the question, Mr Falconi's hand gripped Tyler's dick shaft as Sal continued speaking, "Very nice, indeed…Have you ever modelled before? Maybe you should come work for me…Have you done gay porn?"

Tyler gulped in bewilderment, while Sal stroked Tyler's cock. Truth be told, Tyler desired this strong Daddy's dominance from Sal. Tyler had no aspiration except for his job and his muscles. Hence, Sal's imposing influence was welcomed, and genuinely wanted by this innocent Kid.

Tyler's sweat beads continued dripping off his pecs as Sal's firm grip jerked Tyler's teenaged, hormonal dick through his sexy retro shorts.

"I think someone is enjoying this?" continued speaking Mr Falconi.

"Yeah…But we might get caught," said Tyler as his breathing gasped.

Therefore, Mr Falconi's hand released his grip upon Tyler's dick as he spoke, "I don't think you have to fret…I'm kind of well-known around here at Hawk's Gym and in the Hollywood crowd…Here, let me prove this to you, Tyler."

After rummaging around inside his front pocket, Mr Falconi handed Tyler his business card, as Sal spoke, "I own a one of the biggest gay adult film studios in West Hollywood called MAGNUM…And I'm always looking for new talent…There's big money in it if done correctly and if you follow my direction…Why not? But you will have to audition first."

"Well, thanks, Sal…But, between you and me…I've never messed around with a guy before until now…And as a matter of fact, I'm still a virgin…Because I'm waiting for that special someone," said Tyler, bashfully.

"Tyler, the majority of my highest-paid stars were first-timers in the beginning…So, there's nothing to be embarrassed of…Besides, the perks are unbelievable," spoke Sal.

"Well, if you say so…I might be willing to give it a try…But, how much money are we talking about?" said Tyler as he turned to face Mr Falconi as his bicep flexed unconsciously as if trying to impress Sal even more.

"Plenty…Let's say I have the Midas touch, when it comes to finding lucrative talent…Not to mention all the hobnobbing with the Rich and Famous…Have you ever wanted to walk a Hollywood red-carpet or mingle among the Malibu elite?"

"Hell, yeah…Who wouldn't? Well then, I guess, it's my lucky day."

"You could say that…But before we continue…I must see how willing you truly are…Now, turn and face me, Tyler."

Without warning and taking a page from his former pornstar Floyd, Mr Falconi's index finger rammed into Tyler's mouth; where Tyler's lips instinctively started nibbling Sal's finger, lubricating it with continual tongue swipes.

Tyler's innocent brown eyes fluttered as he viewed Mr Falconi's hairy heaving chest pressing against his own perky nipples. Tyler couldn't help, but to whiff Sal's Daddy scent, triggering Tyler's dick into further firmness. Tyler's rationale was eclipsed by sensual desire as Sal's fingers tweaked Tyler's hardening, wired nipples.

"Tyler, now let me feel that tight hole of yours…Good, Kiddo…That's it, I'm using my lubed-up finger," spoke Sal as his hand clutched Tyler's melony butt cheeks.

Sal's hand roamed across Tyler's ass crevice, swiftly pulling away Tyler's thong to expose Tyler's asshole to the coolness of his fingertip. While they embraced, Sal's lubed finger flicked upon Tyler's virgin hole. Before Tyler could resist, Mr Falconi's thick lubricated finger pushed into Tyler's tight butt. Likewise, Sal heard Tyler moan as his finger's knuckle started to slid inside, gliding right past Tyler's favorite thong.

God, he wasn't joking, thought Mr Falconi to himself.

That's some prime virgin ass…

It needs my Italian cock buried inside.

Flustered and inflamed, Tyler tried his best not to have his cockhead gush, right then and there. Nonetheless, precum started dribbling from Tyler's cock lips, smudging his pink thong and snug retro gym shorts.

God, this was better than finger-fucking himself, thought Tyler as his hand grasped Sal's beefy arm that reached around onto his buttocks.

"Sal, I think we should move…Somewhere private," said Tyler, whose breathing was labored as his butthole started bucking upon Sal's finger.

As Mr Falconi withdrew his finger from Tyler's primed hole, Tyler abruptly felt a void in his stretched-out asshole. Then without any warming, Sal slid his formerly butt-buried finger across Tyler's upper lip; which automatically caused Tyler to sniff his own ass aroma. However, instead of being mad; this essentially stimulated Tyler more.

Sal Falconi calculated his every move, transforming Tyler into a freak.

Sal spoke in earnest, "You're sure of this? Because, you know what's going to happen next? And, that means I'll be your someone special."

"Yes, Sal…I want your cock deep inside of me," replied Tyler.

"Very well, Tyler…Lead the way."

Needless to say, as Tyler scampered to the Men's Locker Room; Mr Falconi followed with a fiendish grin as he too inhaled his finger that had just penetrated Tyler's cherry asshole as business and pleasure would intertwine.

God, what a scent, thought Sal as his cockhead spouted precum again.

This Kid might just be the one to save my bankrupted studio.

Sal's destiny continued as Tyler's locker happened to neighbor his own. There stood Tyler stripping out of his skimpy, precum stained gym shorts, revealing his racy pink thong. Fuck, it scarcely concealed Tyler's virgin asshole that Mr Falconi had fingered moments earlier.

Promptly Sal undressed with lustful intent at the sight of Tyler's booty ass, which initiated Sal's dickhead to seep more precum. Brashly, Sal's head motioned for a nearby gym member to leave the premises asap, which gave Sal the free rein to fuck Tyler's hungry ass, recklessly.

When Mr Falconi approached behind Tyler, Sal spoke, "Pardon me, Tyler…Looks like we're neighbors…What are the odds?"

"Not sure…But let me…" said Tyler, moving to let Mr Falconi pass by.

Nonetheless, Mr Falconi's sturdy hands gripped Tyler's thong upon his hips, holding Tyler in place as Sal's swollen dickhead brushed by Tyler's derrière. Sal's cock shaft traced upon Tyler's ass cheeks until resting amidst Tyler's butt crevice as the Kid's buttocks clamped on cue.

God, he's begging to get fucked! thought Sal with a gleam in his eyes.

"No need, Kiddo; now that we got the place to ourselves…My God, you got one helluva ass," spoke Mr Falconi, whose Italian mushroom-shaped dickhead leaked precum upon Tyler's thong ass strap.

Sal's cockhead nudged Tyler's thong to expose his freshly finger-fucked, gaping asshole. Soon, Tyler experienced Mr Falconi's dickhead starting to force open his virgin ass lips, but without success.

Spontaneously, Tyler turned around to see Mr Falconi wearing nothing, but a smile and his track shoes and white gym socks as Sal's dick tried desperately to pry open Tyler's constricted butthole.

Sal caught Tyler's eyes darting to his Italian heritage hairy chest, that tantalized Tyler. There was something alluring about this older, forty-something, domineering gentleman with his dark tanned muscular fuzzy pecs.

"Are you ready?" asked Sal.

Tyler simply nodded YES.

Sal took his rock-hard dick and spat upon it, lubricating his cock shaft as his dickhead tapped against Tyler's ass crevice.

God, what an ass! thought Sal.

Just the thought of what was happening, caused Tyler a rapid hardon; that penetrated through his pink thong pouch as his balls swung out.

Sal guided his greased-spit hand onto his cock, which aimed directly into Tyler's ass crack, lodging his dick once again upon Tyler's asshole. Meanwhile, Mr Falconi's other hand gripped Tyler's pink thong for supportive and authoritative control over Tyler.

Tyler felt a sudden smoldering sensation of pain around his butthole entrance. Ultimately, Mr Falconi's cockhead burst inside. Tyler couldn't help, but wail in this new-found pleasure. Inchingly, Sal embedded his cock further into Tyler's butthole.

And with that, Mr Falconi's dickhead slithered deep into Tyler's virgin hole. Thus, the experienced gentleman, Sal slowed his cock's movement for a second; so that Tyler could get use to the feeling. Sal didn't want to frighten Tyler.

"Fuck, that's amazing!" moaned Tyler.

"You sure you want more?"

"Yes…Feed me your cock…Sal, give it to me all…Let me feel it."

Then Mr Falconi unrelentingly lunged his thick cock into Tyler's ass.

"Ohh, my God…Your huge…I don't know if I can take anymore?" moaned Tyler.

"Yes, Tyler, you will…It's what you've been wanting," replied Sal.

But how did he know? pondered Tyler.

This was what Tyler desired more than anything; to be fucked, especially raw. To have his butt stretched open to the limits by a cock.

What turned up the pleasure for Tyler was Mr Falconi's brawny chest pressing against Tyler's backside. Tyler felt the warmth of Sal's body over his own as Mr Falconi's stiff dick kept plunging his asshole.

Not to mention the sound of Sal's dick thrust in and out as Tyler groaned, while stroking his own dick sticking out from under his thong pouch. Tyler felt Mr Falconi's cock shaft cramming farther into his own warm and tight asshole with each thrust.

Sal continued speaking as his cockhead wedged deeper into Tyler's butt, "God, Tyler, with a body like yours…I'm sure you seen a great deal of action…I can't imagine being your initial fuck?"

"Yes, Sal…You are my first…And, this is what I've been yearning for…To be manhandled by someone special like yourself," said Tyler.

That's all Sal needed to hear as his grip upon Tyler's thong covered hips dug in, which flared-up his cock prodding into Tyler's tight ass. Sal's cockhead was millimeters from Tyler's entombed prostate, so when Tyler pushed backwards onto Sal's shaft; it activated a new arousal. Tyler leaned against Sal's chest as his cock plowed farther.

"Aah, fuck me…" wailed Tyler, who clutched his locker, while pondering how he had woken as a virgin, hours earlier.

Now, Tyler had a Gay Porn Studio Owner snaking his cock within his cherry-busted ass, and Tyler loved the feeling of their moistened bodies uniting as one! Especially when Sal nibbled upon Tyler's neck and shoulders, which tickled and attracted Tyler.

Bracing his locker, Tyler panted for air as he continued speaking, "Sal, honestly, I'm quite shy…But, I'll to do whatever it takes…I've got will power…Just ask Growers Market, why they kept me as their stock boy?"

"Ohh, Tyler…I can see why…Your ass was made to be admired and fucked," muttered Sal, who had devious opinions about Growers Market as Sal witnessed his own dick slamming into Tyler's angelic ass.

Tyler heard what sounded like more spit as Mr Falconi continued lubing his cock, as it lunged unfathomably further into his butthole.

"Trust me, Kiddo…You're perfect…Now, I intend to breed your ass…Giving you some of my cherished seed," continued speaking Sal.

Down the last row of lockers, anyone would have recognized the skin-smacking sound; indicating Sal Falconi and Tyler's sexual activity. Hawk's Gym locker placements were designed with this in mind; that's why the pricey membership fee eliminated those pesky wannabees.

"Ohh, you're going to breed my ass…I've always wanted to feel cum inside my hole…Tell me when, so I can bust my nuts at the same time."

"I'm getting close, Tyler…"

"Ohh, Sal, your dick is driving me crazy…God, I don't think…I can wait…Anymore…" whined Tyler.

Tyler's head dripped from dampness as he shuddered, causing every muscle to clench in unison; not even taking a breath as his dick squirted cumload after cumload upon the gray painted locker in front of him.

Tyler gasped, while shaking his head; causing his ass to squeeze.

"I'm sorry, Sal…But how is your dick getting bigger?" moaned Tyler.

"Fuck, Tyler…Your ass is like a vice grip…Seizing my dick…Here it goes," groaned Sal, whose dickhead assaulted Tyler's virgin asshole by erupting hot cum volleys that flooded Tyler's asshole; hence, drenching Sal's own dick.

Once again, Tyler was in ecstasy as Sal's furry chest collapsed upon his back before Mr Falconi's breathing started settling down. Occasional Sal's body twitched as he wrapped his beefy arms around Tyler's chest.

Repeatedly, Mr Falconi moaned, "Fuck," while squirting the last of his baby juice.

As Mr Falconi's trembled from climaxing such a cumload, Sal rose off Tyler's backside and patted Tyler's hips as his cock popped out of Tyler's jizz saturated hole. Like a champagne bottle uncorked, Sal observed his own cum starting to trickle out of Tyler's smooth ass lips.

"Tyler, I just wanted to ask…" spoke Mr Falconi as Tyler interrupted him with the most passionate kiss ever.

"Thank you…That was amazing…I'm guessing that was my audition?" said Tyler, whose sweat-soaked body radiated with a mischievous grin.

"Tyler, you promise to call me tomorrow…I have the perfect project for you…Now, I definitely need to take a shower, Kiddo," spoke Sal, wrapping a towel around his waistline seductively.

"Will do, Sal," replied Tyler, who remained seated on the Locker Room bench as Mr Falconi entered the Showers.

Tyler could have sworn that Sal's dickhead bobbed under his towel. From that moment, Tyler was fascinated by Mr Falconi, whose hairy trail crept over his belly button and up his Italian barrel chest until reaching his darkened red nipples. Tyler yearned to tweak those nipples in sexual horseplay, but that would have to wait for another day.

Tyler read Mr Falconi's business card…

Owner and Principal Director of MAGNUM Studio…

Now, this mesmerized Tyler.

So, Sal Falconi did own a gay porn studio? thought Tyler.

Tyler had graduated from high school with no precise direction.

Maybe, this was fate?

Hell, what could go wrong?

Chapter Three – A Star is Bred

After Sal gave the Hawk's Gym Owner an appreciative, yet conniving blowjob; Sal Falconi and Tyler secretly met with his anonymous donor. A demure, but well-off computer programmer known has Mr Haskell.

This unpretentious bachelor seemed too enthusiastic for Sal, for investing into his Magnum Studio. Haskell's appearance was ordinary, but his intelligence level was through-the-roof. Privately, Sal would remark to Tyler that apparently Mr Haskell had apparently no street smarts, hence an easy hustle.

Thankfully, Mr Haskell agreed to bankroll as a silent partner. However, it was Tyler's talented butt that persuaded Mr Haskell to join forces with Sal Falconi, to save his precious Magnum Studio.

Amicably, Mr Haskell got permission to tongue Tyler's bubble butt. However, under Sal's ultimatum; no sexual intercourse would be tolerated, or Mr Haskell would surrender his entire investment.

Now, a fidgety Mr Haskell sat adjoining to the Director's chair inside Magnum Studio's Grand Re-Opening as the film crew scurried about.

Meanwhile, Sal licked the nervous moisture off his lips as his heart raced that a fired Floyd would make a surprised appearance; hence disrupting his filming. And yet, his nerves quelled; knowing that two buff security guards were at the Stage door as he yelled, "Action!"

In his porn film debut, Tyler wore a grey baggy sweatsuit, which didn't emphasize the boy's physique. Instead, Sal wanted to tease the viewer, gradually stunning them with Tyler's hidden chiseled definition.

And back from his retirement in Palm Spring was none other than Casper, whose greying black hair gave him the authoritative look for acting as Tyler's Family Doctor in this medical-theme porno. Not to mention the rise of Casper's colossal ten-inch inches back on screen!

Casper was dressed in a blue business shirt, red silk tie, black trousers, and covered by a white Doctor's lab coat. Wrapped around Casper's neck was a fake stethoscope, emphasizing his portraiture.

Yes, it was Sal's idea to abbreviate Tyler's name to Ty, so he won't miss his cue.

After one-script reading, Casper commenced the scene with "Ty, what brings you into my office today?"

"It's embarrassing."

"Come…Here, jump up on the exam table, and we'll have a look-see."

Tyler positioned himself on the edge of the examination table.

"Ty, I need you to remove your sweatshirt…"

"But you'll laugh at me."

"Nonsense, I've seen it all…"

"Okay, if you say so…You know best."

Tyler pulled off his sweatshirt to display a skimpy scoop tank-top, which Magnum Studio's Costume Designer, Mario, had found in the Ladies section of a thrift store. Obviously, this tank-top justified that Mario was not a fan of Sal's latest boy-toy.

Mario thought, poor Jake was to be Sal's hottest rising star…

Not this barely legal gym bunny titled Ty!

This transparent, threadlike material strained to the point of ripping at the seams. And honestly, Tyler looked sandwiched into this tank-top; which made Mario secretly snicker, especially seeing what was next.

Two quarter-size wet spots dotted the material, revealing Ty's noticeably erected nipples. The teenager's nipples stuck out as if ready to explode. Yet again, the masterfully Make-Up Artist Mario had used a nipple pump upon Magnum Studio's newest star; of which, Mario might have pumped Tyler's tits, longer than necessary.

"Ohh, my…I see what's the problem…" spoke Casper, in a reassuring tone, then Casper continued his dialogue, "Here…Let's remove that top."

The Family Doctor started peeling off Ty's nipple-soaked tank-top as he stared upon Tyler's marvelous pecs. Then, softly Casper caressed Tyler's nipples with a sensual smirk as he started yanking upon each tit.

"I see you've been working hard on your pecs."

Fuck, he's gorgeous! thought Casper.

And not bad for my return to film.

Just look at that sculpted body!

And, his blonde naïveté is adorable.

Undoubtedly, Casper would've known after shooting over one hundred pornos during this fifteen-year span in the Industry.

"Those nipples look amazing! Ty, there's nothing to worry about…However, it does look like your nipples are oozing milk."

"Milk? How could that be, Doctor? I'm a man!"

"I think it's obvious that you are taking growth hormones!"

"How did you know?"

"It's a common side-effect of that medication…Like the yearning to try something sexually new…As well as being extremely aroused to touch…"

"Yeah, I sorta have, but my girlfriend is freaking-out…Because my tits are bigger than hers…Doc, please do something to release me from this pain…I'm begging you."

"Well, then…The only remedy I see fit is to milk your tits! Luckily, you've come to the right place…But, let me lock the door, for privacy."

While Tyler fondled his own nipples in each hand, his head dropped backwards as Casper knelt down to start suckling upon Tyler's nips.

"Wait a second…Is this ethical, Doc? I'm your patient…And only eighteen," asked Tyler with an inviting moan.

"Let me take care of the consequences…Now, let's remove these baggy sweatpants of yours…To give you an in-depth examination."

As the Family Doctor helped disrobe Ty of his pants, his eyebrows rose in delight. Because, Tyler went commando and his eighteen-year-old dick started leaking precum as Casper's hand caressed Tyler's cock.

Casper continued speaking, "Well…I wonder if that taste the same."

Just then, Casper's mouth swallowed Tyler's dickhead and worked his way down the boy's shaft. In surprised ecstasy, Tyler had to grip the examination table, fuck!

Thank God, Sal hired a pro! thought Tyler.

Because Casper is incredible!

Being stark naked, Tyler's sun-kissed, ripped body sweated profusely from the bright lights and from the skillfulness of Casper's blowjob. Casper gasped as he released his mouth upon Tyler's decent sized dick.

"Not bad…But, I have another idea for relieving your pain…If you trust me," continued speaking Casper.

"Sure, Doc…I'm in your hands…Do whatever is necessary."

After instruction, Tyler got on all fours on the examination table with his bootylicious, peach-fuzzed ass cheeks aiming directly at the Cameraman. Mr Haskell was on the edge of his seat as a hardon grew.

Meanwhile, Casper was handed a vibrating butt-plug by Mario from the sideline. Successfully, Sal had experimented on Tyler the night before; therefore, Sal grinned like a Cheshire cat reliving their romp.

"Doc…What's that humming noise?"

"Nothing that you have to be afraid of…I'm going to use a vibrator upon your ass…To stimulate your nipples to milk."

After lubing Tyler's newly shaved ass lips, abruptly Tyler felt the vibrator dive into his butthole, arduously. Tyler could only guess that Casper wanted to expedite this filming because Tyler sensed Casper's sexual attentiveness waning. Earlier in Make-Up, Tyler had overheard Casper mentioning to Mario of getting home before rush-hour traffic.

Although two decades younger, Tyler had a capable convincing trait.

Maybe, Sal hiring this former sex-star wasn't a good idea after all, thought Tyler.

Especially, since he lived a couple of hours away, one-way.

I wonder if I can encourage Casper…

To break Magnum Studio's protocol?

Like I did with Sal?

Those old guys can be gullible.

Like that unsuspecting Mr Haskell.

Just like that, Tyler started lamenting with lust, while his fingers rubbed his rigid nipples. In a frenzy of overacting, Tyler pushed his bubble butt backwards, to match Casper prodding the vibrator around his ass lips before it glided into Tyler's asshole.

"Ohh, Doctor...I think it's working...My tits want to be sucked dry!"

"They'll have to wait a minute for I have a special instrument, just for you, Ty," spoke Casper as he unzipped his trousers.

Promptly, Tyler felt Casper's bare dickhead tapping against his asshole, which intrigued Tyler. Because Magnum Studio's had a steadfast policy regarding its actors' safety. There was no bareback filming, period!

Nonetheless, Tyler spread opened his thighs further, giving this acclaimed Casper a provocative invitation to fuck him, and hard.

"What's that?" timidly asked Tyler, in perfect characterization.

"You'll feel soon enough...Trust me, I'm a Doctor."

Meanwhile, Tyler gasped, letting out a loud an extending pleasurable moan as the Casper's dick was squirted with lubrication as Mario anxiously rolled a condom on Casper's impressive dick. Fortunately, there was a stash of Trojan XL's in a Halloween bowl on the Magnum Studio stage, that had been around for years.

"We're ready, Sal," spoke Mario, while wiping-up his lube drenched hands, and thinking, there's got to be more than this?

Having gotten the "all clear on the set;" Ty proceeded with the perfect "I can't believe my eyes" look as his head turned back to see his Family Doctor naked from the waist down with his raging ten-inch dick swaying.

"Ready Son?" asked the Family Doctor as Casper's award-winning cock shoved into Tyler's butt, making Tyler grunt in searing pain.

"Ooh, ahh..."

"That's it...Let me feel it!" directed Sal from his chair as his little buddy start to stir.

Casper increased his rhythmic strokes, penetrating Tyler's pretty ass from various angles as both the Cameraman and still Photographer clicked away for what seemed like forever.

That's when, Tyler started assessing this new chapter in his life.

This wasn't passionate! pondered Tyler.

Not like what Sal and I have.

And have done!

"Good…I think we got plenty of from that angle…Now, Casper, I want you to sit on the table and have Tyler ride your cock, while you fondle his nipples...Maybe even suck one if possible," instructed Sal.

"This should be hot," squeaked Mr Haskell as he elbowed Sal, while Sal's eyes rolled.

Don't say anything, you'll regret, thought Sal as he simply smiled back.

Eventually in a different position, the Family Doctor tried his best to suck upon Ty's stiff nipples as Tyler bounced wildly upon Casper's cock.

Tyler loved it. When Sal had fucked him from this position, that eventually caused Sal's raw Italian cock squirt inside his moist hole.

God, that's what I want! thought Tyler.

While Tyler leaned upon Casper's mid-aged, immaculate hulky chest; he spoke softly something into Casper's ear. Whatever that was, it instantly turned this renowned pornstar into a piston fuck machine.

What did he say? pondered Sal.

Casper is fucking like a horse!

"Ohh, ahh…Doctor fuck me harder…Yeah, that's it…I want to feel your dick rubbing inside my warm, tight hole…Now, I want you to breed my virgin ass, raw!" hollered Tyler

Sitting stupefied beside with his silent partner; Sal leaned forward on his Director's chair, while his mouth gaped open in disbelief.

"Was this in the script?" questioned Mr Haskell, thumbing the pages.

As Casper puckered his lips around Tyler's rigid nipples, everyone heard a balloon popping sound as the condom ripped open; exposing Casper's famed tubular dick slicing into Tyler's sweet asshole with such an unbridled fury. Casper's new objective: to dump his seed in this moist ass before being pushed aside, and kicked off Sal's Magnum Studio set.

"God, yes…That's my boy…Take my seed…Is this what you've wanting?"

"What the fuck?" mumbled Sal, in contrary to his dick's response.

The Cameraman and Photographer exchanged quick glances before continuing their duties as their own dicks started ballooning.

Hell, even the unscrupulous production assistant, Mario, stopped in place. Thus, Mario's sizeable package swelled in his complimentary Andrew Christian bikini briefs. Which was awkward, since Mario had just disdain for Tyler.

The heat of the scene had enveloped each production crew member to the point that no one intervened with Casper and Tyler's natural heat.

"Doc...I feel you...Give it to me," said Tyler similar to Sal's first-time.

United as one with an abundance of sweat coated their impeccable bodies; they soon shuddered. First, indicating that Casper had spattered his baby-batter into Tyler's astonishing ass; Casper howled ecstatically.

Exhausted from this filming marathon, Casper's glistening body fell back on the exam table as he muttered, "That was freaking amazing."

At last, Tyler sprayed his cumload with stream after stream spewing upon his dazzling moistened abs; while a reinvigorated Casper playfully pinched upon Tyler's bullet-size nipple as they giggled without a care.

Tyler winked back at Sal; having thought, I'll be crowned Sal's new porn star!

His protégé!

"Sal?" nudged Mr Haskell, looking unassured for the first-time.

"That's a wrap!" spoke Sal, who darted from his Director's chair to his private office, where he slammed the door.

What have I done? pondered Sal.

Have I created a monster?

Tyler's ejaculation merged with Casper's breeding, which dribbled from his puffy ass lips; hence puddling the examination table with jism.

In the interim, Casper's burly arm gripped Tyler's chest as the two stayed and took promotional photo shots for this Magnum Studio film.

"Guys, I must tell you…That was fucking HOT!" said the Photographer.

"It was all his fault," grinned Casper, who tousled Tyler's blonde hair strands like frat brothers.

"Yeah, after some coaxing from yours truly," said Tyler with a chuckle.

The two turned and kissed passionately as their dicks regained in girth. Then spontaneously, they laughed; while dueling their dicks.

"Excellent…That's the spirit! God, this is what Magnum Studio has been missing," said the Photographer as his camera clicked incessantly.

Mario lingered in Sal's doorframe, before asking, "Do you wanna talk?"

Sure, Mario was more than a mere Costume Designer/Make-Up Artist and jack-of-all-trades porn set assistant, which included bottoming for a despondent, drunken Sal Falconi when necessary. And secretly supplying the necessary ingredients to his actors, out of eyesight.

"What have I done? I should have stopped it!" Sal spoke, swigging a shot of Whiskey straight.

As Mario approached his Boss, he said, "It's not your fault…Maybe, maybe we can salvage this?"

"Like how? Without ruining our safe-sex practice? Not to mention being banned?"

"Upload it to the internet…Just that scene for sale…At least you could get something out it? But under a New Studio banner like PURE production…Ask your newest buddy, that Mr Haskell to design you a webpage," said Mario, who started massaging Sal's shoulders.

"That's brilliant! And keeps Magnum Studio out of harm's way…What would I do without you…"

You'll never know, thought Mario with a smirk before he gave Sal a peck kiss on his wavy Italian hair; that Mario noticed starting to grey.

In the meantime, Casper had showered, and was now dressed in his casual Palm Springs attire; while Tyler walked out of Sal's office. Looking like a dismayed child, who had a talk-down by the Principal.

"What's up, Ty? Did the great Sal Falconi scold you for barebacking on your first scene?"

"Yeah, you could say that…And he's taking it straight to online streaming…Using a newly formed unknown studio name with the help of that Haskell dude…So, what's the point? No one will see it."

"Trust me…Sal's going to make a small fortune…Just you see…Because, someone here has raw talent…Now, give me a hug."

As the two embraced before Casper departed the Magnum Studio set, Tyler whispered into Casper's ear, "I loved that dick of yours…Not to mention your seed…Anytime you're back in West Hollywood…If me a holler."

"Definitely, I will do…" spoke Casper as he spanked Tyler's athletic rump.

Chapter Four – The Hollywood Insider

In the scheme of things, the all of Magnum Studio talent hustled; and this was expected of them from Casper to Floyd. Everyone was hired for a sexual tryst with Sal Falconi orchestrating it; thus, profiting on the sideline with his share.

If you were pretty, then arm candy at an Award Show. Muscular, then a personal trainer. Able to carry a dinner conversation, a Charmer.

On his way, Tyler fitted perfectly into each category.

However, Tyler's childish inexperience might lead to his downfall, and Tyler realized this. So, Tyler enlisted to learn from the best. After much arm-twisting and having been coerced from Sal Falconi, himself. Tyler would meet-up with Magnum Studio's Bottom of the Year award winner, Vonn, for a candid how to make it in Hollywood Q&A interview. Of course, Magnum Studio would cover the luncheon, but nothing else.

Vonn was a triple threat who ponied his short-lived adult career into TV stardom, playing a caramel skin-toned striking, ripped Adonis; ironically as a Rookie in a Network Cop Drama.

Was this typecasting from his winning scene from "Rookie Does Best"?

Absolutely!

Did this bother Vonn?

Hell, no…when you're making thirty-five thousand an episode.

And, you're having the Show's Producer plowing your ass, whenever that Sugar Daddy needed to release his tension.

Vonn wasn't stupid!

He made sure he got dialogue in every episode, guaranteeing his contractual payment; while giving the Head Script Writer weekly blowjobs. Never piss-off a script writer was one of Vonn's cardinal sins.

Thus, Vonn found himself sitting across from this child by the name of Tyler as they finished-up their poolside lunch at the Beverly Wilshire Hotel. Clearly, the legacy of this spot was lost upon Young Mister Tyler.

God, help me! thought Vonn, who smiled with fake sincerity.

Talk about an award-winning performance!

This Kid's sunglasses came from Walgreens!

At least, He should have attempted to wear a knock-off designer sunglass.

I pray that nobody from the Network sees me.

Now, where's the check?

So, I can get out of here…

"May I refill your water glass?" asked the Latino Bus-boy, who startled Vonn from his train of thought.

"Ohh, yes…Thank you," spoke Vonn.

As the Bus-boy stood there wearing the standardized white uniform, Vonn couldn't help sizing-up the Bus-boy's crotch under his fitted pants.

Well, ain't that impressive, pondered Vonn, as his Southern roots crept-in.

"Been working here long…" inquired Vonn to the Bus-boy.

"No, Sir…I started just a few weeks ago…So, I'm still learning the ropes…Like what the customer wants and desires without hesitating to ask," said the Latino Bus-boy, as the water pitcher tumbled ice cubes.

The Bus-boy's charming, dimple smile made Vonn want to shoot his jizz upon, and those luscious lips!

"Well, I hope they're treating you well."

"Thank you, Sir…It's been good so far…I've got lots to learn…Like where you can hide from the Boss…Since, He can be a real prick."

With his elbow on the tabletop, Vonn spoke, "You don't say…Now, do you got any ideas for hiding me?"

"Excuse me, but I'm conducting an interview here," interrupted Tyler, who glared at the Bus-boy with contempt.

"Tyler, don't get your panties in a bunch…But, he's right…Young Mister Tyler wants to break into the Big Screen, and I'm fortunate to give him some advice of how to make it big…and hard," spoke Vonn, whose hand stealthily squeezed the Bus-boy's firm butt cheek.

"That's very nice of you…Well, then…I should leave you two alone."

"Ohh, before you go…Where is the nearest baño, Dante?" asked Vonn.

While Vonn read Dante's name tag, Vonn gripped his cock for Dante to observe; unseen from Tyler's view under the pink draping tablecloth.

"There's a single stall inside the Piano Bar…That no one really uses…It's nearby…But, I'll have to show you the way," said Dante.

"Perfect! I think we're all done here…I got to hit the Boy's Room…Tyler, tell Sal…Thanks for covering the check…And best of luck on your career," spoke Vonn, who rose from their secluded table.

Hell, Vonn couldn't get up fast enough as he followed behind Dante like two school kids on a treasure hunt; both knew where this was going.

Dante happened upon Vonn's table Waiter, and mentioned that the young gentleman wanted the bill for the meal.

"But take your leisure…" said Dante in Spanish with a wink.

The Waiter acknowledged with a nod.

Dante opened a secured French Door that led from the poolside verandah into the dark polished wood bar surrounded by leather cushioned chairs. As Vonn removed his expensive sunglasses, he sensed the legendary sufficience, while soaking-in every detail from this venue.

This famed Piano Bar was known for A-Listers to be seen, where deals were struck…and Oscar Winners paraded their notoriety.

"Sir, come quickly, this way," said Dante, whose arm pointed into the dimly lit hallway with its stately velvet green wallpaper.

As the Gentlemen's bathroom door burst open, Dante's white uniform top was being peeled off by Vonn, who hurriedly helped to unbutton it. Without delay, Vonn bent over to gnaw Dante's brown, fuzzy nipple. Which was quite a feast, since Vonn towered over Dante by nine inches. Then, Vonn's tongue advanced up Dante's neck until reaching his jaw.

Where, these two kissed like long-lost lovers until Dante broke away.

"I don't have much time, Sir…I got to watch out for my Boss."

"OK…Let's get to the good part," spoke Vonn with his devilish grin.

Faster than a magician, Dante found himself facing Vonn's backside as Vonn's fingers started sliding down his Rodeo Drive purchased slacks. Giving Dante his incentive, Vonn felt his stylish bikini briefs yanked off his buttocks as Dante spread apart this Bottom of the Year winner's ass crevice.

While Vonn clutched the sink basin, Dante's trained tongue started lapping upon Vonn's ass lips, making this former porn star wail with excited anticipation. And craving a sex partner younger than his Producer.

"God, you're good…"

He hasn't seen anything yet, thought Dante as his el diablo desire abound.

Before Vonn could ask if Dante had a condom; he felt Dante's solid dickhead pushing through his ass ring, causing Vonn's mouth to drop as he gasped, while his eyes rolled back.

"Ohh, God…Yes…Fuck my ass…"

"You like that, Sir?"

"Fucking yeah…Give me your Mexican seed…"

As the two wobbled over the sink, Dante propelled his cock further into Vonn's damp, warm hole.

"God, you're beautiful, Sir!"

"So, I've been told…" spoke Vonn with a naughty hint.

"I'm going to give you my babies…You want…Right?"

Vonn was motivated, working his sculpted-indented, caramel skinned ass cheeks. Vonn's hole sieged Dante's cock, milking his dick.

"Give it to me…Hurry…Before anyone finds us…"

"What the fuck is going on here?" asked Dante's Boss.

Sounds of their skin-smacking session muffled the arrival of Dante's Boss, whose aggravation invigorated into eroticism as Dante felt his uniform pants and sexy bikini underwear being tugged down. Then, Dante felt a swift slap upon his cherubic, cocoa-colored, hairy buns.

"God, I've been waiting to fuck your ass, Dante…Here's my chance," asserted Dante's Boss as his brutish, dry fingers jabbed into Dante's hole.

Of course, Dante was a regular line dancer in Silver Lake gay clubs; that marketed towards the LA's Latino community. However, Dante had never bottomed before. So, when Dante felt his Boss's bear-like tummy rubbing against his spine; Dante freaked as his Boss's spit-lubed cockhead started to invade his guarded and untouched asshole.

"No! You can't…I've never…" howled Dante, but it was too late.

Dante's whining essentially stimulated his Boss's rage even more.

With his fingers gripping Dante's shoulders, Dante heard his Boss exclaim, "God, your ass is tighter than my wife's pussy…I should've known when I hired you that you had the perfect ass for breeding."

"Stop! You're hurting me."

"Shut the fuck up! We don't want everyone knowing our business."

Sure enough, Dante's unyielding asshole gave into the pleasures of bottoming. Being sandwiched between this Bear of a Boss, and Vonn with his alluring Hollywood charm; Dante decided to liberate his libido.

"Ohh, fuck…What's happening? You okay, Dante?" inquired Vonn, who sensed Dante's dick surging in its thickness.

Once again, Vonn's eyes flickered uncontrollably; rolling backwards as he held onto the sink with dear life, while his dickhead pounded under the sink's bowl; seeping precum. Vonn feared that their fuck session would wreak havoc, pulling the basin from the wall.

"Fuck, Dante…That ass of yours is one tight Mother…" declared his Boss as his pelvis clapped against Dante's jiggling, angelic buttocks.

That's when, Dante pressed backwards against his Boss's padded potbelly as he leaned his face rearwards to obtain a sloppy kiss. Of which his married Boss obliged. Nonetheless, while their tongues intertwined, Dante sensed his stout arms being pulled back. Like when being arrested, Dante's wrist was apprehended behind his neck.

"You liking that? You fucking wetback…You enjoy it…When the Cops come to search your bod?"

"Yeah, Boss…Fuck, my hole…Give me your American seed."

"Now, we're talking…"

But before Vonn could voice his criticism, Dante's thrusting cock shaft discharged his jism, pouring Vonn's asshole with hot cum seed. Dante's body convulsed as his own butthole clutched upon his Boss's dick.

"Ahh," forewarned Dante's Boss in what seemed like a never-ending grunt.

As his Boss collapsed upon Dante's small frame, Dante sensed his Boss's dickhead dumping the last of his seed.

God, what a feeling, pondered Dante.

"Who's this?" quizzed Dante's Boss as his cock popped from Dante's sweet ass, that started seeping his cumload.

"A customer…"

"Who's got a nice ass…And just look at that dick…C'mon, Son…Why don't you spew your load over Dante's hungry lips?" jostled the Boss.

While resting upon the basin, Vonn stroked his awe-inspiring dick.

What a shame that he's a bottom, thought Dante as he crouched in front of Vonn's jerking cock shaft.

And yet, that was common in the Gay Porn Industry; big dick bottoms!

Nonetheless, Vonn wailed like his life was in jeopardy as his cockhead gushed, cum ropes across Dante's lips and face, and even in his shiny black hair. As Vonn trembled, both himself and Dante's Boss witnessed Dante's lips cleaning every morsel from Vonn's cum spray dousing.

"Well, that didn't take long…Did it?" said Tyler, who happened to bump into Vonn exiting the Piano Bar.

"Like I said earlier, Tyler…You must enjoy it, while you can…Because this Business will eat you alive…Oh, and don't forget to say hi to Sal for me," spoke Vonn, who's shirt was obviously untucked from his backside.

Tyler smirked seeing a wet spot nearest Vonn's asshole.

Lucky, son-of-a-bitch, thought Tyler, who quickly pivoted.

"Excuse me, young man…Watch where you're going!" announced a recently checked-in, three-piece business-suit attired, polished baldheaded Executive that Tyler unintentionally had walked into.

"Ohh, I'm sorry, Sir…Honestly, I didn't see you there…" said Tyler.

"Well, now that you see me…What do you think?"

"Not bad…Guess you're traveling alone?"

"This trip, I am…By the way, how old are you?"

"I'm old enough to be in porn…Why don't you lead the way."

"You better call your Daddy, and tell him…You're running late."

And with that, the golden-leafed elevators closed; having Tyler and his latest acquaintance ascend to the Penthouse Level as the Executive's hand clasped Tyler's bubble butt.

Chapter Five – A Fast Learner

Tyler was instructed to take a shower. A very soapy shower, cleansing every nook and cranny. The sudsy kind that makes your body linger with the fresh scent from the bar of soap. Afterwards, Tyler was requested to join this Business Executive on the bed; naked, of course.

While Tyler dropped the damp towel on the marble bathroom floor, he started primping himself in the beveled mirror. Admiring his defined bod. Like his hefty pecs and that bubble butt, which were a thing of beauty. And his blonde hair; of which, this Executive had none.

Yup, a complete bald Mother-fucker, thought Tyler.

Which made this Executive, alluring in his own way.

Tyler cracked the bathroom door open; he noticed a pitch-dark bedroom. Both intrigued and yet, scared. Tyler's eyes squinted to find his way.

Hell, the only glimmer of light came from Tyler leaving the bathroom door ajar. Tyler even hollered, making sure that the Executive was still there.

"Over here, Boy," replied the Executive with his deep voice.

Ernie was there alright. Ernie, aka this Business Executive, had just flown-in from New York City, and was raring for the company of this puppy-eyed, Tyler. Luckily, Ernie's baldness shimmered in the light.

As Tyler approached; he could detect a faint image of nude Ernie, seated on the bed. Ernie looked be to stroking his cock in earnest.

"You smell really nice, Boy…" continued speaking Ernie.

"Thanks"

"And from what I'm feeling…You got a fine cock, that needs attention."

"Yeah, I guess so…"

"Come, here…Have a seat, while I'll suck your cock."

Just like that, Tyler stretched-out on the luxury linen, his back rubbing upon the fabric as if confirming its coziness in a catlike manner.

I could get use to this, thought Tyler, who realized Sal's frugalness might drive him away.

Ernie found his way between Tyler's legs; where he grabbed Tyler's cock and placed it upon his lower lip.

His tongue swirled around Tyler's dickhead. Before inhaling Tyler's entire cock shaft down his throat, where Ernie's nose brushed against Tyler's trimmed pubic hairs. Which nearly tickled Tyler.

Tyler smirked, thinking that Ernie could possibly choke on his dick. Nevertheless, Ernie kept bobbing up and down. Thus, surprising Tyler with his blowjob skills. Every now and then, licking Tyler's smooth balls.

Fuck, Ernie's got game! thought Tyler.

So much so, that Tyler informed this sexual obsessive Ernie that he was close to cuming.

"God, this has been amazing...But, I think we should hold for a sec...You know, before I bust my nuts," said Tyler.

 Ernie's mouth did release from Tyler's dick; however, he was just starting as his tongue swiped upon Tyler's piss slit.

God, such youthfulness, pondered Ernie.

Ernie spoke authoritatively, "Here, let me push your legs back...Grab them with your arms...Yeah, that's it, bring them up closer towards your chest...Now, show me that bubble butt of yours...You got a fine ass, Boy."

This time, Ernie savored Tyler's dangling balls, while his saliva drooled; puddling in Tyler's pink puffy asshole. While Tyler pressed his legs towards his chest, Tyler felt Ernie tracing his finger around his shaved ass crack.

Which caused a sudden spasm on Tyler's outer ass ring.

"Ohh, that's driving me crazy...Fuck, my dick is leaking...Whatever you're doing...Keep going..."

Immediately, Ernie buried his finger in Tyler's butthole.

Tyler was shocked for a moment, but then Tyler's ass ring got used to Ernie's finger, fucking his butthole.

Looks like someone is enjoying this, thought Ernie.

"I told you…You've got a sweet bubble ass…And that hole is precious."

Tyler groaned as his dick had a mind of its own. Tyler gripped the linen, while his toes curled. Meanwhile, his back felt glued to the linen.

"Sorry, Ernie…I can't hold it back…Any longer…" wailed Tyler.

That's when Ernie pulled Tyler's rigid cock between his legs as Tyler shot his teenage cum into Ernie's fervent mouth. Every single seed of Tyler, got gulped in Ernie's gullet.

While Tyler's athletic and sweat drenched physique clutched every muscle, Tyler had just realized that he had never cummed like this before.

Hell, Tyler swore he had flashes in his vision like fireworks.

"Fuck" uttered Tyler as his dick turned sensitive to Ernie's touch.

Tyler's blinking eyes stared at Ernie, while he pushed his legs down between Ernie. Although wedged between Tyler's sturdy legs; Ernie felt a sense of tranquility from this fascinating youngster that he attained from the Lobby with ease.

He swallowed all my cum, thought Tyler.

Without hesitation…

Now, that's some freaky dude.

And, why was it seemingly more so with baldies?

Feeling totally spent; Ernie started inching over Tyler's torso until he stopped. Then Ernie's hands took turns rubbing each of Tyler's manly nipples, pinching and waiting for a wicked response. That's when Ernie's butt straddled over Tyler's swelling cock shaft.

Tyler knew that he had to get Ernie off, and the quicker, the better.

Especially since, Tyler didn't want a lecture from Sal upon their return home. Once done, all Tyler had to do; was give Sal a call to be picked-up from the Hotel.

Besides, what was the point of me being here? thought Tyler.

Ernie's mature, married ass started bucking over and over Tyler's shaft like a pole dancer. Which rejuvenated Tyler's dick.

Then Ernie spoke, "Boy, I want you to fuck me."

While Tyler cupped his fingers behind his head, flexing his biceps; Tyler grinned, while Ernie continued to beg Tyler to fuck him.

"Come on, now…What's Daddy got to do?" continued speaking Ernie.

This was a first, and honestly, Tyler really wasn't sure that he wanted to do this. Tyler had never topped before, since bottoming was so natural.

Nonetheless, Ernie moaned and pleaded for Tyler's dick.

"Trust me, Boy…I'll make it worth it for you," spoke Ernie.

"Okay…Go ahead, ride my dick…But don't tell anyone about this."

Ernie made a playful shh-pose with his finger, while his other hand gripped Tyler swelling dick.

Fuck! His hole is lubed already! thought Tyler.

He came prepared.

Tyler sensed Ernie's ass descending over his cock shaft as his asshole engulfed Tyler's teenage dick. More than anything, Ernie wanted to trip Tyler's boyish hormones into a blissful savage fuck session.

God, he's tight! thought Tyler.

Of course, who would have known?

That this strait-laced Business Executive took cock up his ass?

And I did notice his wedding ring.

Soon enough, Tyler found himself balls deep in Ernie's butthole.

Which, feels moist and warm, thought Tyler.

"You want to breed my ass?" spoke Ernie.

"Yeah…"

"I can't hear you, Boy."

"I'm going to breed your hole...Daddy."

"That's Daddy's good Boy."

"Fuck, it feels amazing…"

"Yeah, you always wanted to fuck your Daddy's hole."

"Ohh, Daddy."

"Come on, Boy...Give it to your Daddy...Fuck Daddy's ass."

Tyler couldn't believe how good it felt. However, Tyler fantasized that it was Sal Falconi instead of New York, Ernie jockeying upon his cock.

Which caused Tyler to fuck Ernie hard, and wanting to fuck him even harder. Ernie moaned, while jerking himself off. That's when Ernie squirted his jizz over Tyler's sun-kissed, chiseled chest.

Fuck, Ernie's cock shot a load so huge that a couple of volleys landed upon Tyler's handsome chin and lips. Of which, Tyler's tongue wiped with his lips with no reluctance.

God, that taste pretty good, thought Tyler.

The rest of Ernie's load either dribbled down Tyler's chest, running onto the silky sheets or pooled between Tyler's mound-shaped nipples.

After tasting jism on his lips, Tyler yearned to taste more cum. Thus, Tyler arched his back upwardly as he tongue-mopped his chest cleaned.

This was beyond believe for Ernie; never had a hustler ever done that before!

"You're fucking gorgeous," spoke Ernie in awe of Tyler's naughty exploit.

"You don't say...You're pretty hot yourself, Daddy."

Between the daydream of fucking Sal, and having Ernie hovering on his cock shaft; Tyler couldn't resist shooting another load, but this time inside Ernie's ass as Ernie leaned over to give Tyler a passionate kiss.

"Fuck, you just literally exploded in my ass...Now, that's what I call a wow factor..." spoke Ernie.

Tyler felt Ernie's ass ring clench upon his shaft, draining every droplet.

"A wow factor? I've never heard that before..."

"God, you're so naïve...I've got lots to show you...If you're interested?"

While Tyler didn't say a word, an exhausted Ernie collapsed on the bed top beside Tyler. As Ernie's fingers caressed Tyler's leg, then his pelvis; slowly galloping over each ab row of Tyler before grasping a smooth pec in his palm.

"You honestly don't know who I am?" asked Ernie.

"No, I'm sorry...But you can tell me if you wish," said Tyler.

Mission accomplished! thought Tyler with a grin.

"I'll have my Studio's Casting Director call you for an audition, first thing tomorrow morning…Don't be late…And dress to impress…Like you did with me…Now, it's time for you to scoot along," spoke Ernie, closing the suite's door to the corridor.

With a twinkle in his eye, Tyler phoned Sal to inform him, that he was ready to leave.

While he maundered through the opulent Beverly Wilshire Hotel Lobby, Tyler was too exhilarated to notice the shadowy figure; following closer in a rapid pace, gaining fast upon him.

"Hey, hey," yelled this figure.

Annoyed at the catcalling, Tyler turned to see who this could be.

Tyler said, "What are you doing here? In a place like this?"

Before Tyler got his answer, he felt his bicep being tugged with a strong force, pulling him out the side door; and away from Sal's approaching vehicle at the Hotel's front entrance.

As Floyd spoke, "Business…Just like yourself…We'll got plans to discuss, privately."

The Epilogue

Sal looked at this watch as he circled the Beverly Wilshire Hotel Lobby for the twentieth time. There was no sense in calling, because Tyler's cell phone went straight to voicemail.

Where the fuck was, he? pondered Sal.

In a secluded corner, Sal called Vonn. However, as each ring was unanswered; Sal's frustration level rose.

"You'll reach Vonn…Sorry, guys…I'm not available right now…"

Sal ended the call.

This is ridiculous! thought Sal.

Sal popped his head into the Piano Bar. Taking one last look around until his eyes caught those of this burly, baldheaded gleeful gazing guy at the end of the Bar; who had this look of smug satisfaction, all to himself.

Sal strolled passed the leather cushioned, occupied swivel stools. Soon, Sal stood next to this rough in years, but charismatic-looking, out-of-town Executive type. The type that frequents the adult bookstores, and partakes in gloryholes, while away on business.

"Looks like you're enjoying yourself?" asked Sal.

"You could say that," he spoke, while taking a swig of Whiskey.

"I wouldn't mind...Some enjoyment, myself," spoke Sal.

"Ohh, you don't say?" replied Ernie.

Ernie's swivel stool turned to face Sal's side, while Ernie's hand grazed over Sal's Italian crotch with intimacy.

Then Sal spoke, while facing Ernie, "So, how did my Boy, Tyler, do?"

"Excellent...Except for forgetting to collect," mentioned Ernie in disappointment as he dropped the wad of bills on the bar counter.

"Fuck! He's that immature? Maybe, he's not ready for the big leagues? Should we reconsider?"

"Fuck no, Sal...Tyler is quite teachable...Not to mention, remarkable in bed as you should know...Besides, he's got the best trainer in Hollywood," spoke Ernie, raising his glass to Sal.

"Then, where the hell is, he?"

"Got me...We finished-up nearly an hour ago...Maybe, he decided to walk home, instead?"

"That's what I'm afraid of...He doesn't know this area well," spoke Sal, who surveyed the Bar; praying to catch a glimpse of Tyler.

Tyler's butt ring felt a singed sensation as this colossal cylinder cock bore deeper into his magnificent bubble butt, raw and with barely any lubrication.

"Ahh," moaned a stripped-naked Tyler, whose asshole started responding to this conquering cock.

"Fuck" uttered Tyler in a soft-tone.

Tyler did not want to give any indication, that his butt was being gratified by this beast of a cock.

With each thrust, broadening his butthole further; Tyler's body glistened with sweat. Then without warning; it happened. Tyler's butt started bucking back over this intense black dick, aching for more.

"Ohh, fuck…Breed my ass…Do whatever you wish," squealed Tyler.

Now, Tyler's hands reached over his butt cheeks, and pulled them apart. Thus, accepting Floyd's phenomenal cock.

With his eyes reddened, his black coal-skin dripping with moisture, and his admired and envious dick prodding profusely into Tyler's virgin black-dick, fucked asshole.

Floyd spoke, "You sure…You're getting all of this?"

"Got it!" replied Mr Haskell, while jerking his own oscillating boner from his pants.

Fuck that MAGNUM STUDIO! thought Mr Haskell

And that Sal Falconi…

This will make me a fortune.

Meanwhile hidden behind Mr Haskell, stood a smirking Mario.

THE END

About the Author

After numerous rejections for my suspense thriller; my neighbor said to me, "Write what you know."

Little did she know, how mischievous my sexual adventures had been.

I have lived the majority of my life in Las Vegas, where I continue to work at the Major Strip casino.

I was blessed when I met my future husband, whom I have been together with for over thirty years. And, yes…he's twenty years older than me.

My husband has been my rock during hard times, and although he may call my erotica writing "just a hobby."

I hope to give my Readers the best in erotic storytelling.

Thank your encouragement.

Regards,

Naughty Tommy

The Naughty Tommy Collection of Erotica

- Coach's Lust*

- Rhythmic Thrust

- The HUNG Juror*

- Compromised Lust

- Freakie Friday*

- Seducing Coach*

- Bareback OPS: Nubian Prince

- Wicked Privilege*

- Discovery Voyage: Lust at Sea

- Aroused Suspicion*

- Dirty Ambition: Abbott Ranch

- Jock Addiction: The Dean's List

- Bareback OPS: HIS Majesty

- Hollywood Hustle: Innocence Lost

*part of the Wildwood Bareback Series

Printed in Great Britain
by Amazon